Max the Magnificent

by **Trina Wiebe**

Illustrations by **David Okum**

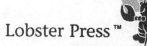

Lobster Press ™

To my critique buddies, a talented group of women and a wonderful source of support — Amy McAuley, Leslie Carmichael, Alma Fullerton, Lisa Marta, Gloria Singendonk, Lori Robidoux, Laurie Brown and Serena Chea. Thanks a million! — Trina Wiebe

Published in 2008 by Lobster Press™
1620 Sherbrooke Street West, Suites C & D
Montréal, Québec   H3H 1C9
Tel. (514) 904-1100 • Fax (514) 904-1101 • www.lobsterpress.com

Publisher: Alison Fripp
Editor: Jane Pavanel
Graphic Design & Production: Tammy Desnoyers

We acknowledge the financial support of the Government of Canada through the Book Publishing Industry Development Program (BPIDP) for our publishing activities.

We acknowledge the support of the Canada Council for the Arts for our publishing program.

The Canada Council | Le Conseil des Arts
for the Arts | du Canada

Library and Archives Canada Cataloguing in Publication

Wiebe, Trina, 1970-
     Max the magnificent / by Trina Wiebe ; illustrations by David Okum.

(Max-a-million, 1701-4557 ; 1)
ISBN 978-1-897073-94-0

     I. Okum, David, 1967- II. Title. III. Series: Wiebe, Trina, 1970- .
Max-a-million ; 1

PS8595.I358M39 2008   jC813'.6   C2008-901095-7

Printed and bound in Canada.

Text is printed on Rolland Enviro 100 Book, 100% recycled post-consumer fibre.

Table of Contents

1 Max's Plan

Max wanted to be rich.

Absolutely filthy, stinking rich. He wanted to have more money than he could spend in ten lifetimes, and he wanted it all before his twelfth birthday. Was that really so much to ask?

"Why don't you buy a lottery ticket this week?" Max suggested to his dad.

Dad looked up from his computer, where he'd been typing at top speed and muttering under his breath. "What's that, son?"

"A lottery ticket," Max repeated. Dad got pretty spaced-out when he worked on a story. Sometimes Max had to say things four or five times. "Why don't you buy a lottery ticket this week?"

"Darn . . . frozen again," groaned Dad, staring at the computer screen. "Why on earth would I want to buy a lottery ticket?"

"So we can win the jackpot," Max explained slowly, as though speaking to a child. "I hear it's a big one this time."

"Lotteries are a waste of money," said Dad. He stabbed the enter key repeatedly. "Nobody wins those things."

Max knew this wasn't true. He saw the winners on TV all the time. They looked so happy, holding those gigantic checks with the long line of zeros on them. Lots and lots of zeros.

"You can't win unless you buy a ticket," Max said. He reached over and touched the escape key. The monitor came back to life.

Dad smiled. "Hey, thanks. I've got to get this article done today and the computer has been driving me crazy." Dad worked at the newspaper and was always facing urgent deadlines.

"Lottery tickets are only a few dollars," prodded Max. "What do you say?"

"Forget it," Dad said, finally turning his attention to his son. "What do you need all that money for, anyway? If you're saving up for something special, maybe you can do some extra chores around here. The garage needs cleaning."

Max frowned. The garage smelled gross, like the last person who'd cleaned it had died in

there. Besides, it was full of spiders. "No thanks," he said. "Just think about the ticket, okay?"

Max went outside and sat on the front steps. He thought about asking his mom to buy a lottery ticket, but decided against it. She was out in her flower garden tending her prize-winning delphiniums. She wouldn't want to be interrupted. Sometimes Max thought the best way to get

Mom's attention would be to turn green and grow leaves. Anyway, she'd probably say no, too. Max loved his parents, but he could see they weren't going to be any help when it came to getting rich.

Max's family wasn't exactly poor. Dad made a decent salary at the newspaper and Mom worked part-time at the public library, so there was always enough money for boring stuff like food and clothes. But when Max asked his parents for something cool like the night-vision goggles he'd seen at Ed's Outdoor Megastore, the ones with four levels of photosensitivity and an operating distance of 600 yards in starlight, the answer was always the same.

"Sorry, Max, too expensive. Why don't you save up for something a little more ordinary, like binoculars?"

That was the problem. His whole life was ordinary. He had nice, ordinary parents who lived in a nice, ordinary house and drove a nice, ordinary car. And the funny thing was, they seemed to like it that way.

But Max knew, deep down, that he was meant to be a millionaire.

There was his name, for one thing. Maximillian J. Wigglesworth III. It was a rich name. It practically screamed money. Someone with a name like that should have three fancy cars parked in his garage and pour champagne on his breakfast cereal instead of plain old milk.

"I hope Dad doesn't think I'm greedy," Max said to one of Mom's garden gnomes sitting three steps below him. He picked up a rock and tossed it at a bird feeder hanging from a nearby branch. It missed, landing in the grass with a thud. "Because I'm not. I'll build homes for the homeless, feed the hungry, even cure a few diseases. And I'll buy an enormous mansion for Mom and Dad that has a cook and a butler and a moat."

His parents could quit their jobs. Claire Wigglesworth would become world-renowned for the exotic orchids she'd raise in the solarium she'd finally have, and Maximillian II would become a famous travel writer and take Max on explorations of the ancient pyramids of Egypt. And with any luck, if they didn't have to work so hard, they'd pay more attention to him.

Max tossed another rock and this time it hit the bird feeder, making it swing wildly. Maybe the lottery ticket wasn't such a wonderful idea. But Max refused to give up. He knew he was destined to have tons of money. He just had to find a way to get it.

2 The Amazing Albertini

"Hey, Max. Wha'cha doing?"

Max lifted his chin off his knees at the sound of the voice. When he saw who it was he plopped it down again.

"Hi Sid," he said. "I'm just thinking."

Sid grinned. "I thought I recognized that zombie look on your face." She leaned her scooter against the house and sat down beside Max.

Sid's real name was Serendipity Sunshine Stubberfield, and she hated it. She hated it so much that at the age of four she'd changed her name to Sid, refusing to answer to anything else. Nobody at school knew her full name except Max, and he'd been sworn to secrecy.

Max didn't mind keeping Sid's secret. The kids at school would tease her forever if they knew her real name. Max knew what it felt like to be teased. Going through life as Maximillian J. Wigglesworth III wasn't always easy.

"Where's my bag of gumballs?" Sid asked,

holding out her hand.

Max leaned down and grabbed a brown paper bag out of the garden gnome's plastic wheelbarrow. He handed it over with a smile.

Sid was addicted to gum, the chewier the better. She liked crunchy candy-coated gum, squirty gum in a tube, and exploding gum with goo in the center. But her all-time favorite was gumballs.

Unfortunately, the only kind of gum her parents let her chew was sugar-free and dentist-approved. Sid detested it. So once a week she gave Max some of the money she earned working at her parents' store. This week she'd instructed him to buy an assortment of sugary gumballs guaranteed to rot the teeth.

Sid buried her freckled nose in the top of the bag and breathed deeply. "Ahhhh, thanks." She chose an extra-sour green apple gumball and popped it into her mouth, then offered the bag to Max. "You're the best."

"No problem." Max picked out a large one with blue and yellow speckles and put it in his pocket for later. Chewing would interfere with his concentration, and right now he needed to concentrate.

Sid blew a fat green bubble, then pinched the end of it. The bubble collapsed, plastering itself to her chin. "So what are you thinking about?" she asked, rolling the sticky bits into a ball and popping it back into her mouth. "You look like someone ran over your dog. And you don't even have a dog."

"I'm trying to come up with a plan," he said. "I need to get rich quick."

Sid snorted. "Not that again."

Max looked offended. "What do you mean?"

"Come on, Max. You're always plotting to get money," Sid paused to blow another bubble. "Remember the root beer?"

"Oh, that." Max grinned. Last summer he'd decided to develop his own top-secret recipe for root beer. After weeks of experimenting with molasses and yeast and sarsaparilla root, he'd poured the dark liquid into bottles and left them in the basement. Late one night, every last bottle had exploded. The neighbors had called the police, thinking they heard gunshots.

"And don't forget the time you borrowed your dad's three-hole punch and went into the confetti business," added Sid. "How many stacks of old newspapers did you go through before you realized nobody wanted to buy grungy gray confetti?"

Max held up his hands. "Okay, okay, enough." Mom was still finding little circles of paper when she vacuumed. "Maybe those ideas weren't so great."

Sid giggled. "I can't wait to hear your new scheme."

"I don't have one yet," sighed Max. "I've been thinking about it for days. If I could just come up with the perfect plan, I know I could make loads of money. Then all my worries would be over."

"What worries?" demanded Sid. She tugged at the brim of the Brooksville Batters baseball cap she always wore. She chomped her gum furiously, reminding Max of a pitcher about to throw a fastball. "You get good grades at school, your hair is a decent color and you have normal parents. You can't possibly have any worries."

Max had to admit this was all true. Sure, Mom spent way too much time talking to her plants and Dad zoomed off into outer space whenever he was working on a story. But they were normal compared to Sid's parents.

"You won't believe what Bliss made me for breakfast," said Sid, rolling her eyes. "Zucchini pancakes." Sid's parents insisted she call them by the names they'd chosen for each other on their wedding day. Which wouldn't be so bad if they were regular names, but how many kids had to introduce their parents as Ziggy and Bliss?

Sid's parents were different in lots of ways. They owned a tiny shop downtown where they sold things like unbleached toilet paper and tofu wieners. They dressed weird too. Sid's dad was fond of tie-dyed vests and her mom wore dangly earrings she made herself from recyclable materials like bread bag clips, drinking straws and aluminum pop can tabs. You had to be careful when she leaned forward to hug you or you could lose an eye.

"Well, I still want to be rich," Max said. "So are you going to help me think up an idea or what?"

Sid blew another bubble and held it while she thought. Then she popped it. "What about a paper route?" she suggested. "Your dad works at the newspaper. I'll bet he could get you a job."

Max shook his head. Delivering papers sounded about as exciting as cleaning the garage. "Nah, that's small potatoes. You've got to think big, Sid. I want lots of money."

Sid wrapped a pumpkin-colored curl around her finger and tugged on it. "You could raise rabbits and sell them for pets," she said with a smile. "I know where you can get organic carrots real cheap."

"Think bigger," Max said. "You can't get rich selling rabbits. Unless," he paused, raising one eyebrow, "unless they were specially trained. Then I could charge a hundred dollars a rabbit. I'd make a fortune."

Sid looked doubtful. "Housetrained rabbits?"

"No," groaned Max. Why did he always have to explain his ideas to everyone? "Trained, Dippy, as in tricks. You know, like being pulled out of a hat or disappearing into thin air. That kind of thing."

"Don't call me that," said Sid. She paused, then squinted thoughtfully at Max. "But you don't know anything about magic."

"I wish I did," grumbled Max. "Then I could conjure up a truck full of money. Presto, wham-o! Instant millionaire."

"Yeah, that'd be cool," agreed Sid. She suddenly sat up straight. "Hey, did you hear that the Amazing Albertini is coming to town? He's the best magician in the whole world. I'd pay anything to see one of his shows. I heard he turned a monkey into a banana, and one time he . . ."

Max didn't hear the rest. He was stuck on three words: *I'd pay anything.*

Sid was right, people would pay anything for tickets to see their favorite rock band or movie star. Or magician.

3 C for Costume

"That's it!" shouted Max, leaping to his feet.

Sid stared at him. "Huh?"

Max grinned and pointed skyward. "To the attic!"

Sid sighed, grabbed her bag of gumballs and obediently trotted after him into the house. Up in the attic Max headed for a wall stacked high with cardboard cartons. They were all neatly alphabetized.

"What are you looking for?" asked Sid.

Max didn't answer. He walked along the boxes, running his finger over the labels. It didn't take him long to find the one he wanted.

"Voila!" he cried. He stopped in front of a large carton labeled "C – Costumes." It was right where it was supposed to be, between "B - Baby Clothes" and "D – Dishes." Mom organized everything. It was one of the side effects of being a librarian.

Max had been a wizard for Halloween last year, and if he knew Mom, his costume would be stashed away with every other costume he'd ever worn.

He opened the box.

"Presto," he crowed, pulling out a silky red cape. He gave it a shake and inspected it carefully. A few of the glittery lightning bolts and silver sequins had fallen off, but even in the dim attic it sparkled and shimmered.

Handing the cape to Sid, he dug deeper in the box. He came up with a slightly crushed top hat that had been part of his circus ringleader costume when he was nine. A little more digging produced the elegant black cane that went with it. He plopped the hat on his head, tapped the top of it smartly with the end of the cane, and sneezed as a cloud of dust enveloped him.

Sid sneezed too. "What are you going to do with that goofy outfit?"

"My cape," Max demanded. He flung it around his shoulders and turned to admire his reflection in a dusty mirror. "This goofy outfit is going to make me rich."

"It is?" Sid didn't sound convinced. "How?"

"Allow me to demonstrate." Max plucked the hat off his head with a dramatic flourish and bowed deeply at the waist. "Ladies and, er, Sid. May I introduce the most amazing, astonishing and absolutely astounding magician the town of Brooksville has ever seen. The one, the only . . ." Max paused, thinking hard.

"Mighty Max?" suggested Sid.

Max shook his head. That made him sound like an out-dated cartoon character. Or a toilet bowl cleanser.

"Magic Max?" tried Sid again.

That was better, but still not quite it. Max needed something flashy, something catchy, something totally mind-blowing. He grinned as the perfect name came to him.

"Max the Magnificent!"

Sid clapped her hands. "Bravo," she cried, "bravo." Then she frowned and backed away as Max tossed the cane high into the air and caught it with practiced ease. "Not this again," she muttered.

Last summer Max had gone into the baton

business, making beautiful batons decorated with glitter and tinfoil. He'd even given lessons, teaching the Thompson sisters two doors down how to spin and twirl. Unfortunately, his most brilliant inspiration – fire batons – had set the Thompson clothesline ablaze, putting an end to his baton-twirling days.

Now, wearing a stage smile so wide his cheeks ached, all of Max's moves came back to him. He twirled the cane faster and faster. Round and round it spun, whooshing as it cut through the air. Then his fingers slipped.

"Watch out," he cried.

Sid belly flopped onto the attic floor. Her cap flew one way and she rolled the other, instinctively protecting her head with her arms. The cane hurtled through the air and struck a box marked "W – Winter Woolens." The box teetered, then fell forward and burst open, burying Sid in a jumble of scarves, mittens and outgrown sweaters.

"Sorry, Sid," laughed Max, digging through the tangled heap. He grabbed his friend by the

elbow and pulled her up. "I guess I need to practice."

Sid glared at him. "You think?"

Max grinned sheepishly. "You'll help me, won't you? Every magician needs an assistant. Please?"

Sid bent down and picked up her cap. She looked at it, grimaced, and shook off a dead moth before plunking it back on her head. "I don't know, it sounds like a dangerous job. You're not going to cut me in half, are you?"

Max didn't answer. His eyes had that distant look again, the one that meant that his brain was crackling with electricity, working out the details of his latest plan.

He had his costume and his assistant. Now all he needed was a magic act.

4 Setting the Wheels in Motion

Max's cape billowed behind him as he thundered down the attic stairs.

"Mom," he hollered. He never worried about making too much noise. A herd of elephants could stampede past his mom and she wouldn't notice, especially if she were involved in one of her hobbies. She became preoccupied sometimes, just like Dad. There were days when Max felt practically invisible.

"Mom," shouted Max again. He raced past the bathroom and through the living room, his top hat flying off his head as he rounded the corner. No Mom. He sped through the dining room and toward the kitchen, hoping to find her making lunch.

Max pumped his arms, enjoying the rush of air on his face. Then his socks hit the kitchen floor and his legs shot out from under him. Suddenly he was hurtling like a bobsledder across the linoleum.

"Aaaah," he yelled, trying to steer himself between the wall and the kitchen table. His ride ended with a thud at the base of the refrigerator. Mom stood next to the stove with a recipe book in one hand.

"Is that you, Max?" she asked, studying the book, then slowly stirring the thick, pale liquid that bubbled in the pot.

Max got to his feet and straightened his cape with as much dignity as he could muster.

A lightening bolt drifted to the floor. "Mom, I need a favor."

"Hmmm?" she murmured, still reading and stirring. Max peered under the book to see the title. "Flipping for Fondues," he read out loud. He glanced over at Sid in the doorway, who shrugged.

"I had no idea there were so many different kinds of fondues," said Mom. She dipped a finger into the pot and licked it. "Mmm . . . very good. You know, most people make cheese fondues like this one, but you can also use vegetable broth, hot oil, chocolate or marshmallow."

"I've decided to dedicate my life to the art of deception," Max jumped in when she paused to take a breath. "I'm going to be a world-class magician, a master of illusion." He realized Mom wasn't listening. That was nothing new. He took a deep breath and tried again. "Just call me Max the Magnificent from now on."

"Sure," said Mom. "You know, you can dip just about anything. Fruit chunks, bread cubes, meatballs, chopped vegetables . . ."

Max decided to give it one more try. "I've got my costume and my lovely assistant . . ." He was interrupted by a choking noise from Sid, which he ignored. "Now all I need is my act. Does the library have any books on . . ."

Mom finally looked at Max. "Books?" she repeated. "Well, of course, honey. I'll have to check the junior non-fiction section, but I'm quite sure we've got a number of books on magic tricks. I'll bring some home with me after work tomorrow."

Max grinned. His career as a magician was off to a great start. He'd just mastered the trick of getting Mom's attention, hadn't he?

Opportunity Knocks

"Boring, boring, boring," grumbled Max the next afternoon. He was lying on his bed, thumbing through one of the many books on magic Mom had brought home from the library.

"These tricks are for little kids." He slammed the book shut and tossed it on the floor with the others. He'd been through each and every one, some of them twice. They had titles like *Simple Magic Tricks* and *Astound Your Friends in Three Easy Steps*.

He rolled over and glared at the ceiling. "I'll never get rich with these stupid books."

Well, he had to admit that they weren't all stupid. *101 Knotty Knots*, a book on rope tricks, had some neat stuff in it. Like how to cut a rope in half, then magically make it whole again. Nothing that would make him rich, though. The book on Harry Houdini was kind of interesting, too, but it didn't give away any secrets. And that's what Max needed, the secret to at least one great trick.

There was a knock at the door and Dad stepped into the room. "Who are you talking to, son?"

"No one," said Max. He didn't sit up. He was too depressed.

"Did you sort out your money troubles?" asked Dad.

Max groaned. "I don't have any money. That's the whole trouble."

"Well, I'm off to do an interview," Dad said. "Why don't you come along? It might cheer you up."

"Uh, no thanks, Dad. I'll just stay home. I've got a lot of thinking to do."

Max had gone on interviews with Dad before. They were boring too. Mostly they involved a lot of sitting around and listening. Two of Max's least favorite activities.

Dad shrugged. "Suit yourself. I thought you might enjoy meeting the Amazing Albertini, but if you're too busy . . ."

The Amazing Albertini?

Max was at Dad's side in two seconds flat.

"Are you serious? Wait till Sid hears about this!"

Dad chuckled. "I thought you might change your mind."

"Can Sid come too?" Max asked, following his dad down the hall. She would owe him big time for this.

Dad hesitated. "Well, I'm kind of in a hurry."

"Please?" begged Max. "Sid is a huge fan. She'd kill me if I got to meet the Amazing Albertini and she didn't."

"Okay, okay. Give her a call." Dad stopped in the kitchen and searched his pockets for his car keys. "But tell her to be ready. We'll pick her up on the way."

Max grabbed the phone and quickly dialed Sid's number. She took the news exactly as he'd expected, whooping so loudly at the other end of the line that he had to hold the receiver away from his ear.

"Come on, Max," called Dad from the front door. "We can't keep the Amazing Albertini waiting."

Sid lived four blocks away. Her house was easy to spot because it was the only one on the street with a "natural" yard. In this case, natural meant overgrown. The grass was so tall in some places that it almost reached Max's waist. It provided a healthy habitat for birds and insects, Sid had explained with a pained expression.

Halfway to Sid's house they braked for a red light. Dad was muttering under his breath. Max couldn't make out the words, but he suspected it had something to do with the interview. When Dad balanced his notebook on the steering wheel and began scribbling furiously, Max knew he'd been right.

Beep! Beep!

"The light's green," Max said. The car behind them honked impatiently. Max grabbed the pen and notebook. "Earth to Dad. C'mon, drive."

"Right." Dad glanced in the mirror at the traffic backed up behind them and stepped on the gas. Soon he was muttering again.

Max shook his head. Whenever Dad

worked on a story it was all he thought about. Sometimes it bugged Max, but today he was too excited to care. For once, Dad's job was working to his advantage. An interview with the Amazing Albertini! How perfect was that?

Max's brain hummed. He'd been going about this all wrong. The best magic tricks wouldn't be found in books that anybody with a library card could sign out. Those were ordinary tricks. Max needed something extraordinary.

And for that, he had to go directly to the source.

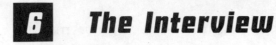

6 The Interview

"I can't believe we're actually going to be in the same room as the Amazing Albertini," gushed Sid as they climbed the steps to the theater. "This is the most exciting thing that's ever happened to me!"

Max wasn't paying attention. He was excited too, only for a different reason. This was his big chance to meet a real magician. And if all went well, learn the secret to a super fabulous trick. One that would make him tons of money.

Max grinned as they entered the lobby. He could almost smell the money now. Or maybe that was stale popcorn he was sniffing. Either way, he knew he was hot on the trail of his future wealth.

"The dressing rooms are backstage," Dad said, leading them down the center aisle. Empty seats spread out on both sides of them.

"Do you think he'll give me his autograph?" asked Sid. She fumbled in her pocket and pulled out a wrinkled paper. It was a leaflet advertising the magic show. The Amazing Albertini and his assistant, the Lovely Lola, smiled up at them. Perched on Lola's shoulder was a small monkey. Sid giggled. "Maybe he'll even shake my hand!"

"You'd better let me do the talking," Max said. Sid was practically drooling. If she kept this up the Amazing Albertini wouldn't take them seriously. And he wouldn't give Max the information he needed so badly.

Max knew this wasn't going to be easy. Magicians never revealed their secrets. His only chance was to convince the Amazing Albertini that he needed to become a magician to fulfill his destiny. Max was prepared to get down on his knees and beg if he had to.

Max and Sid followed Dad backstage. They walked down a narrow hall where the paint was cracked and peeling. Finally they stopped in front of a door with a leaflet taped to it, identical to the one in Sid's hand.

Dad knocked twice. The sound echoed in the empty hallway. It seemed odd to Max that they hadn't seen anybody. Where was the Amazing Albertini's entourage? Where were the stagehands and lighting guys and press people? Surely a famous magician would be surrounded by dozens of helpers and admirers.

Dad knocked again and the door swung open.

"Enter," commanded a voice.

They stepped inside.

"Is this it?" whispered Max, taking in the cramped, windowless dressing room. It was nothing like he'd expected. No crystal chandeliers, no expensive flowers, no velvet lounging chairs. The few sticks of furniture he could see were drab and shabby.

Max studied the room. Maybe it was stuffy and ugly, but it was filled with all kinds of cool things. There were brightly colored hankies, gleaming silver rings, giant playing cards, coils of shiny crimson rope . . . every surface was piled high with props and costumes.

But no Amazing Albertini.

"Hello?" called Dad. He looked at Max and

Sid and raised his eyebrows. "Mr. Albertini?"

"Welcome," boomed the voice.

Max craned his neck but couldn't spot a body to go with the voice. Sid nudged his arm, her eyes bright with excitement.

"He's invisible," she whispered.

Dad cleared his throat. "Uh, Mr. Albertini? I'm Max Wigglesworth from the Brooksville Times. I phoned earlier about an interview. I was hoping to ask you a few questions."

"Sit," instructed the voice. "I'll be with you momentarily."

Dad hesitated, then stepped around an enormous steamer trunk to sit in the only spot available, a worn loveseat covered in an itchy-looking brown fabric. He balanced his notebook on his knee and clicked his pen, ready to take notes. Sid brushed past Max and plopped down on the other half of the loveseat.

Max frowned. There was no way he was going to stand there for the whole interview. He knew from experience how long Dad could talk. It would be tight, but he'd rather be sandwiched between Dad and Sid than stuck standing in the doorway for the next hour.

"Move over, Dippy," he hissed at Sid, edging his way around the trunk.

"Hey, watch it," she hissed back as he accidentally stepped on her foot. She gave him a shove. "I'd like to keep my toes, thanks."

Max shoved her back. "If your feet weren't so big I wouldn't have stepped on them."

"Knock it off," warned Dad. But it was too late. Sid jerked her foot free and pushed Max at the same time. He flapped his arms, lost his balance and crashed backwards onto the trunk.

"Oomph," said a voice.

Max froze, half-sprawled on the lid of the trunk.

"Would you two stop fooling around?" Dad frowned and pulled Max to his feet. "I wouldn't have brought you along if I'd known you'd act like this."

"Sorry," Max said. He squeezed between Sid and his dad, keeping his gaze on the wooden trunk.

"Not another word," warned Dad.

Max tried to sit still. If there was one thing he hated, it was waiting. Seconds ticked by. Giving up on the trunk, he looked around the room, wishing the magician would hurry up and appear.

After a moment his nose twitched. "Do you smell something?" he whispered to Sid.

Sid jerked her thumb toward the opposite corner of the room. "I think it's coming from over there."

On the floor beside a dressing table was a tall, rectangular shape draped in a white sheet. At the very bottom, where the sheet didn't reach, Max could see wire bars and bits of straw. He looked more closely. Bits of straw and animal droppings. Grimacing, he switched to breathing through his mouth.

Suddenly there was a thunderous roar and a cloud of blue smoke filled the room. When it cleared the Amazing Albertini was standing before them.

7 Monkey Business

"Bravo," cried Sid, "bravo!"

Max waved blue smoke away from his face. Appearing out of nowhere! Now that was a trick he definitely needed to learn.

The magician towered over them, his shiny boots planted on the lid of the trunk. He flung his arms in the air and his long black cape rippled behind him.

"The Amazing Albertini, at your service," he announced in a deep, rich voice.

Dad coughed. "Max Wigglesworth from the Brooksville Times. Good to meet you."

"Ah, yes. I'm always happy to speak to the press." The last of the blue smoke disappeared and the magician reached into his cape and produced a furry brown ball. He chuckled as the ball slowly uncurled itself. "May I introduce my talented monkey . . . Shimmy."

"Is that the monkey you turn into a banana?" asked Sid. "He must be the smartest monkey in the world." She stared at Shimmy like a starstruck fan. Max jabbed her in the ribs before she could do something foolish, like ask for the animal's autograph.

The Amazing Albertini smiled. "Shimmy features in many of my performances. Perhaps you'd like to pet him?"

Dad cleared his throat. "Actually, sir, I just have a few questions . . ."

"Eieee! Eieee!" Shimmy bared his pointy teeth. Then he climbed onto the magician's shoulder and jumped across the room to land on the cage. He squatted there, picking things out of his fur and popping them into his mouth.

"Yeah, he's a genius," Max whispered to Sid, pointing at the snacking monkey. Immediately, Shimmy snatched up a juggling ball and fired it at Max's head. Dad gasped and ducked behind his notebook. The ball bounced off the wall and turned into a dove, which flapped away harmlessly to perch on the dressing table. For the first time Max noticed that the floor was polka-dotted with bird droppings.

"Shimmy," chided the Amazing Albertini.

He climbed off the trunk and wagged his finger at the monkey. "That's no way to treat our guests." He pulled out the dressing table chair and sat facing Dad. "Pay him no mind."

Dad lowered his notebook, keeping a wary eye on the monkey. Shimmy stuck out his tongue and blew a loud, sloppy raspberry.

"Er, well," began Dad, opening his notebook and flipping through the pages. "First of all, I wanted to ask you . . ."

Max tried to concentrate on the questions, but it was hard. He wasn't interested in how many cities the Amazing Albertini had traveled to or where he'd trained to be a magician. Max only had one question.

How could he become rich and famous too?

While Dad asked questions and took notes, Max found himself staring at the magician. The cape and the trunk had made him appear majestic, but now it was easy to see he was shorter than Dad. Older, too. There were wrinkles at the corners of his eyes and Max noticed that the bottom of his cape was frayed.

It must be his practice cape, thought Max. Someone that rich probably had a whole closet full of brand new outfits.

Pins and needles crept up Max's calf. He counted the tiles on the ceiling. He stuck out his tongue at Shimmy and considered pointing at him again to see what the monkey would do. Anything to make the time go faster.

Suddenly he couldn't stand it one minute longer.

"You've gotta help me, Mr. Albertini," he blurted out. "I need to learn magic, fast!"

8 A Change in Plans

Dad glared at his son. "I'm so sorry, Max has forgotten his manners . . ."

The Amazing Albertini raised one hand, silencing Dad. He leaned forward and studied Max. "You sound desperate."

Max ignored the dirty look Dad was shooting at him. He spoke quickly. "Yes sir, I am. You see, I've decided to become a magician like you and make a mountain of money. I just need one really fabulous trick to start with. And since you've got so many, I thought maybe you wouldn't mind sharing one with me. You know, one magician to another."

The Amazing Albertini sat back in his chair, making a tent under his nose with his fingertips. "Well, I have to admit, my chosen profession has made me wealthy beyond my dreams. It would be only fair of me to give something back."

Max sucked in his breath. Was this it? Was his wonderful plan about to be realized?

"However," continued the magician, "what

you're asking is impossible. You have to under-stand that once a magician gives away his secrets, the illusion is gone. Without the illusion, the magic just becomes a trick. People don't want to be tricked. They want to be amazed, astounded and astonished."

"But . . ."

Dad cut Max off. "I think our interview is over," he said, prying himself out of the loveseat. He leaned forward and held out his hand. "Thank you for your time."

The Amazing Albertini stood and shook Dad's hand. Then he offered his hand to Max.

Max forced himself to respond. Discourage-ment settled in the pit of his stomach like a heavy meal. All of his wonderful plans were ruined.

Instead of grasping Max's fingers however, the magician reached behind his ear. "For you and your friend," he said, presenting Max with two tickets. "I may not be able to share my secrets, but I can share a magical experience. Front row seats, too," he added with a wink.

"Thanks," said Max dully. He shoved the tickets into the pocket of his jeans. Head down, he followed Dad and Sid to the car.

"I'm disappointed in you Max," said Dad as they drove to Sid's house. "That was incredibly rude. Mr. Albertini is a professional and deserves to be treated like one."

"I'm sorry," Max mumbled. He knew if he didn't apologize now, Dad would go on forever, like some of his editorial pieces in the newspaper. Besides, the last thing Max needed was a lecture. He slouched lower in the back seat.

Dad glanced at Max in the rearview mirror. His frown softened. "Well, at least you got free tickets to the show tonight."

Max pulled the tickets out of his pocket, leaned past Sid and dropped them on the front seat. "You take them. I don't want to go."

Sid gasped.

"I've already got a ticket," said Dad. "I'm covering the show for the paper."

"Well I want to go," declared Sid. She slugged Max on the arm. "This show has been sold out for weeks!"

Max rubbed his arm but didn't answer. He turned and stared at the passing street signs. How could he watch the Amazing Albertini perform his act, knowing all the while that he, Max, would never be a magician? He'd come so close today, sitting in that dressing room, surrounded by all those wonderful, mysterious props.

Max sat up a little straighter. An idea buzzed in his brain, an idea that might solve all his problems. If he could get his hands on some of those props, maybe he could figure out their secrets on his own! All he needed was a few minutes alone with them. After reading all those library books, Max had a good idea of what to look for.

It wouldn't be wrong, exactly. Magicians invited members of the audience to come on stage all the time. They were needed to make sure the hat was empty or the rings were whole. It was all part of the act.

The only difference this time was that Max wanted to inspect the props in private, up close and personal.

9 **Time for Action**

"Wow," said Sid that night, "this place is packed!"

"It looks like the whole town is here," agreed Max. The theater hummed with excitement. People moved up and down the aisles, finding their seats and talking and laughing.

"Where did your dad go?" asked Sid.

Max shrugged. "He's probably interviewing someone. He said he'd meet us at the car after the show."

Sid tucked a strand of hair under her baseball cap and grinned. "I'm glad you decided to come," she said. "These seats are amazing. I can't believe how close we are to the stage. It's all so thrilling!"

Max nodded. Sid didn't know it yet, but things were going to get a lot more exciting before the night was over. He glanced at his watch, eager for the curtain to rise.

The house lights dimmed and a hush fell over the crowd. Sid squeezed Max's arm and settled back in her seat. Max glanced at his watch.

Timing was everything. The dressing room had to be completely deserted.

The curtain gave a jerk, then rose. A spotlight stabbed through the blackness, lighting center stage. For a moment nothing happened. Then, with a deafening clash of cymbals and a puff of blue smoke, the Amazing Albertini appeared.

The audience burst into wild applause. Haunting flute music filled the theater as the Amazing Albertini raised his arms and produced his assistant in a cloud of red smoke.

Max stopped clapping and stared. It was the Lovely Lola. She was even more beautiful than her picture on the leaflet. The spotlight danced over her glittering costume and shiny blond hair. He wondered why they hadn't seen her earlier, at the interview.

"Wow," whispered Sid. "She's gorgeous."

With another clash of cymbals the performance began. Max analyzed every movement the Amazing Albertini made. He studied the Lovely Lola's full skirt and decided it wasn't just for

show. Magicians were always hiding things up their sleeves.

Fifteen minutes into the performance, Max tapped Sid on the shoulder. It was time.

"What?" she hissed.

"Follow me," he whispered. "I need your help."

Sid frowned. "Now? But the show . . ."

Max tugged on her sleeve. "Yes, now. It's our only chance. I'll explain later."

"But . . ."

Max put his finger to his lips. This was the tricky part. They needed to slip away quietly, without being spotted. If anyone asked, he would say they were looking for the washroom.

Luckily the audience seemed to be in a trance. No one noticed Max pull Sid through the side door that led backstage.

10 A Daring Idea

"Have you lost your mind?" demanded Sid, jerking her arm free.

Max glanced down the dimly lit hall that led to the dressing room. It was empty. He hoped it stayed that way.

"Just the opposite," he whispered. "I've had a brainstorm! All I have to do is get into the Amazing Albertini's dressing room. I know if I can examine his props I can figure out how some of the tricks are done."

Sid shook her head. "No way, Max. This is too crazy. It's breaking and entering. It's trespassing. It's insane!"

Max grabbed her wrist before she could turn and run. "I'm not going to do anything wrong," he insisted. "I just want to look around. No one will even know we were there."

Sid chewed her lip. "What if the door's locked?"

"Then we'll go straight back to our seats. I promise."

Grumbling, Sid allowed herself to be towed the rest of the way. When they arrived at the dressing room, Max held his breath and reached for the doorknob. If it was locked he could kiss his dream of becoming a magician goodbye. He wrapped his fingers around the cold knob, drew a deep breath and twisted.

The door swung open.

"See," Max whispered, "he can't be too worried about his stuff if he didn't even lock the door."

Sid grunted.

Max slipped inside. He didn't dare turn on the light in case it drew attention. He glanced over his shoulder at Sid.

"Dippy, come on," he urged. "You'll be seen for sure out there."

Sid hesitated, then scurried into the dressing room. Max tiptoed across the floor, the hair on the back of his neck prickling. He glanced around, half expecting someone to jump out at him.

"Okay," he said softly, "you're the lookout. Let me know if you hear anyone coming."

Frowning, Sid nodded. She hovered near the open door, poking her head into the hall every few seconds to make sure it was empty.

Max knew he didn't have much time. Soon it would be intermission and the Amazing Albertini might return. If he was going to learn something, he'd better do it quick. He blinked impatiently as he waited for his eyes to adjust to the dark.

"Something's different," he mumbled to himself. Then it hit him. All the best props were gone. Max groaned and slapped his forehead with the palm of his hand.

Suddenly he felt foolish. He must have been nuts to think the props would be here instead of on stage. He and Sid were missing the show for nothing.

"Come on, Sid," he muttered. "Let's just go."

Sid whirled around, white-faced. "Someone's coming!"

11   *Trapped*

Max felt dizzy. Panic rippled through his body like an electric shock. "Hide," he croaked.

Sid's eyes were round with fear. "Where?"

Max noticed the trunk he'd fallen against during the interview. He was certain the Amazing Albertini had been hiding in it. If it was big enough for a grown man, it was big enough for them. He grabbed the latch and heaved the lid open. "Quick, in here."

The footsteps grew louder. Sid gulped and climbed into the trunk. "There's no room for you," she whispered.

Sid was right. Her arms and legs seemed to take up all the space. That's not possible, Max thought, but there was no time to figure it out. "I'll find another spot," he answered, already lowering the lid into place.

Shimmy's cage was still covered with the sheet. He darted across the room and slipped between the cage and the wall just as the footsteps stopped outside the dressing room.

Max squeezed his eyes shut and tried to stop shaking. He heard a switch being flicked, then the click of shoes against the floor as someone entered the room. Max slowly opened one eye.

The room was flooded with light. Max peered around the edge of the cage, afraid to breathe or even blink.

It was the Lovely Lola.

Max stared at the woman who'd appeared onstage in a cloud of red smoke. Could it be the same person? This Lola wasn't beautiful.

Her face was covered with a thick coat of stage makeup. Deep frown lines radiated from her mouth. Max noticed that her costume, so glittery and glamorous in the spotlight, had been repaired in several places. Clinging to her neck was a furry brown ball.

"Back to your box, you nasty critter," she said, her voice flat and hard. "Come on, you know the routine."

Max's heart thudded wildly when he realized what she was about to do. He watched, paralyzed, as her high heels click-clicked toward him. She was so near he could smell her heavy perfume. He shrank into the corner.

"Get in there," said Lola, lifting the front of the sheet. Shimmy squawked indignantly as she pried his hands off her, then the cage door clanged shut.

A fine sweat broke out on Max's forehead. He was in trouble now. Maybe he could hide from Lola, but wouldn't Shimmy notice him?

Max tried to recall what he knew about monkeys. Did they have a good sense of smell? Sharp hearing? He slowed his breathing, afraid the slightest sound would give him away.

Suddenly he felt a pain in his shoulder. And another and another. It was Shimmy jabbing him through the sheet. Then two slender fingers pinched his arm. Max clamped his hand over his mouth to keep from crying out.

Shimmy pinched him again and began chattering excitedly.

Max bit back another cry. He had to do something, fast. Remembering the gumball Sid had given him, he dug into the pocket of his jeans and pulled out a handful of stuff.

Did monkeys chew gum?

Shimmy pinched him a third time. As quietly as possible, Max pulled up the bottom of the sheet and slid everything into Shimmy's cage. Maybe that would keep him busy.

Max held his breath. A penny pinged against the bars of the cage and fell to the floor. Then there was a crumpling noise as Shimmy discarded Max's favorite baseball card. Finally Max heard the sound he'd been hoping for.

Chomp, chomp, smack!

Max blew out a silent sigh of relief. Chewing had never sounded so good. He made a mental note to treat Sid to a huge bag of gumballs when they got out of here.

With Shimmy temporarily occupied, Max dared to peek around the corner of the cage. Lola had her back to him. Max inched sideways, straining to get a better view. Lola seemed to be adjusting the many folds in her skirt.

Then, to his horror, she bent over the trunk and lifted the lid.

 12 Disappearing Act

The trunk lid creaked as it swung open.

"Come on, hurry up," muttered Lola to herself. She glanced at her watch. "Show's almost over."

Max was sure his pulse rate had just doubled. Why wasn't she yelling at Sid? Why was she just standing there?

Max heard Lola's skirt rustle, then she dumped some things into the trunk. They rattled and clanked against the wood. Finally she closed the lid, leaning over it until it clicked shut. She grabbed a crimson bundle off a shelf and stuffed it into a fold in her skirt.

"Now for my final act," she said. She surprised Max by laughing, but it was a short laugh that didn't sound happy at all.

When she turned, Max saw that her lips were pressed into a thin, red line. Walking briskly, she left the dressing room. He waited until the sound of her footsteps faded, then slid out of his hiding place.

"Sid?" he whispered. His throat felt dry and tight. "Sid? Are you okay?" Only then did he wonder if the trunk was airtight. Had Sid suffocated?

Max rushed over to the trunk. He grabbed the lid and yanked. Nothing happened. He struggled with it some more before he noticed the latch. With a sinking feeling he realized that the clicking sound he'd heard had been a metal padlock snapping shut.

Sid was trapped.

"Sid," he cried, dropping to his knees. "Sid, can you hear me?"

He almost didn't catch the faint reply. He froze, hoping the noise would come again.

"Max?"

"You're alive," cried Max. He pressed his ear to the lid. "What happened? Why didn't she see you?"

Sid's voice was muffled but Max could hear a note of panic in it. "Get me out of here!"

Max fumbled with the padlock. If he were Houdini, he could pick the lock blindfolded with one arm tied behind his back. But he was just ordinary Max and he needed the key.

"I can't," he told her. "It's locked."

"What?" Sid frantically began pounding on the inside of the trunk, making the padlock thud against the wood. "Max, if you don't get me out of here, I swear . . ."

"I'll get you out," Max promised. "Even if I have to tell Dad the whole story. Can you, uh, breathe?"

The pounding stopped. "Yes."

Max sighed with relief. "Hang on," he told her. "I'll go get help."

He dashed out of the dressing room, not caring how much noise he made. He had to find Dad and confess his whole stupid plan.

Max wondered again why Lola hadn't seen Sid, but then he burst into the theater and all thoughts of his friend flew out of his head. The audience was in an uproar. The house lights were on, the stage curtains where pulled shut and people were milling about in confusion. Several police officers roamed through the crowd, asking questions and taking notes.

"My wallet is gone!" shouted a red-faced man.

"My pearls," cried a woman in a silk suit. "They're missing!"

A little boy near Max tugged on his mother's skirt. "Mommy, I saw a monkey," he insisted.

"Not now, Sweetie," she told him, searching the seat cushions. "I can't find my bracelet. My beautiful diamond bracelet!"

The boy stuck out his tongue at Max and giggled. He scratched his armpit and danced around his mother, who was frantically digging through her purse.

Finally Max spotted Dad. He'd know what was going on. Max wove through the crowd, ducking under elbows and squeezing between seats.

Dad looked relieved when he saw Max. "Oh good. I was looking for you."

"What's going on?" asked Max.

Dad started writing in his notebook. His pen flew over the paper. "Front page news, that's what. Where's Sid?"

"Yeah, well, about Sid . . ." began Max.

"Take her to the car and wait for me," Dad interrupted. "I can't leave now. This could be the biggest scoop of the year."

"But . . ."

Dad was gone. He'd taken off after a police officer, pen and paper in hand. Stunned, Max watched him disappear into the crowd. Was this all some kind of insane dream? Sid was locked in a trunk and the whole theater had gone crazy. Nothing made sense.

Max ran after Dad. When he finally caught up to him, the police officer was speaking.

"I've never seen anything like it," he said, taking off his hat and rubbing his closely cropped head. "I've got thirteen robbery victims, and more lining up to have their statements taken. But not one eyewitness. It doesn't seem possible."

"So you've got no leads at this time, Officer Todd?" asked Dad, scribbling furiously.

"Nothing yet."

"What about the Amazing Albertini? Have you questioned him?" asked Dad.

Officer Todd put his hat back on, his mouth set in a grim line. "Unfortunately, the Amazing Albertini and his lovely assistant seem to have pulled a disappearing act."

13 A Knotty Situation

Officer Todd's portable radio crackled. He raised it to his mouth.

"What?" he barked.

There was a hiss of static, then some garbled words. Officer Todd frowned and clipped the radio back into place.

"We found them," he said, heading for the stage. "It's time to answer a few questions."

Dad hurried after him and Max wasn't far behind. He still didn't know what was going on, but it didn't really matter. All he could think of was Sid locked in that trunk.

They climbed up a set of stairs and slipped through the curtains. It was quieter back here, the noise from the audience muffled by the thick velvet fabric. Max glanced around curiously. Some of the props were still onstage. Nearby stood a tall pedestal holding an empty birdcage.

"Over here," called a female officer, gesturing from the right wing.

"Good work, Perkins," said Officer Todd.

He strode toward her, still trailed by Dad and Max. They stepped around a pile of crates and stopped.

"Whoa," said Max softly.

The Amazing Albertini sat on the floor, holding a cloth to his head. His assistant, the Lovely Lola, huddled next to him. Blood trickled between the magician's fingers and down his forehead. Suddenly Max wasn't sure he was cut out to be a magician. Maybe there were more important things than being a millionaire. Like staying alive.

"I need to ask you a few questions, Sir," said Officer Todd. He cleared his throat, "if you're up to it."

Albertini nodded, then clutched his head and groaned. "Of course."

Officer Todd pulled out a small pad of paper and Dad flipped to a new page in his own notebook.

"Did you get a good look at the suspect?" asked Officer Todd.

Albertini started to shake his head, then

groaned again. "No. I was heading for the dressing room after the show. I was worried about my assistant. She didn't return for the grand finale and I had to finish with the doves instead. Then someone hit me from behind. That's all I remember."

Max heard a gentle cooing noise. He tipped back his head and spotted two gray doves perched in the rafters. Something plopped on the floor, leaving a whitish blob. It reminded him of the dressing room floor. He jiggled Dad's elbow.

"Dad," he hissed, "I have to tell you something."

"Later," shushed Dad.

"What about you, Miss," asked Officer Todd, addressing the Lovely Lola. "Can you give me a description?"

Lola's tears had streaked her mascara and left black lines on her cheeks. "I put Shimmy in his cage during the juggling act, like I always do. When I returned for the finale, I was grabbed from behind, tied up, gagged and blindfolded.

I struggled, but the rope was too tight."

She began to sob again, sending fresh rivers of makeup down her face. Max noticed her wrists. They were rubbed raw. On the floor lay the crimson rope that had been tied around them. There was something familiar about it.

"It's true, sir," said Officer Perkins. "There were so many knots in the rope that we had to cut her loose."

"Who would do such a thing?" muttered the Amazing Albertini. "A blasted coward, jumping people from behind."

"So your assistant was tied up here, on her way back for the final act," said Officer Todd, consulting his notes. "Then, after the show, you left this way as well. Did you attempt to call for help when you found her bound and gagged?"

Albertini wrinkled his forehead. "No . . . I didn't see her until after I regained consciousness. She was lying beside me. I thought she was . . ." he broke off, unable to finish the thought. "I yelled for help, and that's when the officer arrived."

Officer Todd's expression didn't change as he jotted something on his pad. "Officer Perkins found the two of you lying side by side on the floor. Are you sure you didn't see Lola before the assault?"

There was a pause while the magician tried to remember. He shook his head. "I'm positive."

Max stared at the rope near Lola's feet. Where had he seen rope like that? His brain buzzed the way it did when he was on the brink of getting a brilliant idea. Quietly at first, then more insistently. Something wasn't quite right here. If only he could put his finger on it.

101 Knotty Knots. A crimson bundle shoved into the folds of a poofy skirt. And the words,

Now for my final act. Not our final act, or even the final act. *My* final act.

Everything clicked into place.

"Dad," he whispered.

"Just a minute." Mr. Wigglesworth's pen scratched frantically in his notebook.

Max stood on tiptoe to bring his mouth closer to Dad's ear. "Dad," he said insistently.

"Not now, Max." *Scratch, scratch, scratch.*

Max snatched the notebook away. Dad stared at his empty hand for a moment, then turned to Max. He seemed surprised to see him standing there. "I thought I told you to go to the car."

"Yeah, but Dad, I've got to tell you something."

Dad frowned and took his notebook back. "You shouldn't be here, Max. It's not safe."

Max was tired of being brushed off. "Would you listen to me for once?" he demanded.

Everyone stared at him.

Max took a deep breath and continued, "I know who the thief is and I know where she stashed the loot!"

"She did it," declared Max. He raised his arm and pointed at Lola. He didn't how she'd done it, but he was certain she was the one.

"Max, what on earth are you talking about?" asked Dad.

Max held his ground. "She did it," he repeated.

"Surely you're not going to listen to this boy," cried Lola, her eyes wide with shock. "It's utter nonsense. Oh, I feel dizzy." She trembled, her hand on her forehead, then slumped against the Amazing Albertini.

"Now, son, that's a very serious accusation," said Officer Todd. "You can't say something like that without hard evidence."

"It's all the excitement." Dad put a protective arm around Max. "My son's imagination sometimes works overtime."

Max shrugged the arm off. "I'm not imagining anything. I know she did it. And I can prove it."

Lola jumped to her feet. All of a sudden she didn't look faint anymore. "I won't sit and listen to this nonsense. I've just been through a horrifying ordeal! I demand to see a doctor." Her voice rose to a shrill shout. "Immediately!"

Officer Todd looked at Max kindly. "Do you have any physical evidence to back up what you're saying?"

Max shook his head. "No, but . . ."

"See?" cried Lola. She swayed toward Officer Perkins, who was forced to grab her. "I can't take much more of this. It's been such a shock to my system. This child is obviously a liar. Even his own father admits it."

Mr. Wigglesworth held up his hand in protest. "I said he's imaginative, not a liar. If my son says he knows something, then I believe him."

Max shot Dad a grateful look. "I'll show you where she hid the stuff," he told Officer Todd.

"This had better not be a joke," warned Officer Todd. He looked at Officer Perkins and motioned to Lola and Albertini. "Bring them along. I don't want anybody leaving before we get this settled."

"This is outrageous," objected Lola. "My lawyer will hear about this."

Max led the way. When they reached the dressing room he had a sudden awful feeling. What if he was wrong? There were still things that didn't make sense. Like why Lola hadn't kicked up a fuss when she saw Sid in the trunk. And how she managed to rob so many people when she was busy performing onstage.

But it was too late to turn back now.

Max walked up to the padlocked trunk. "In here."

Lola abruptly stopped protesting. The color drained from her face as her gaze flickered between Max and the trunk.

"How do you know this?" questioned Officer Todd.

Max swallowed hard. "Well . . ."

"This dressing room is private property," Lola said in a tight voice. "No one is allowed back here during a performance. You should arrest him for breaking and entering."

"Max wouldn't do anything like that," said Dad. He looked at Max. "Right Max?"

Max looked at the floor. "The door was unlocked," he began. The excuse sounded weak, even to his own ears. "I'm sorry."

"See," said Lola. She smiled coldly. "This child can't be trusted. Officer, here is your thief."

Officer Todd wasn't convinced. "It seems there's only one way to get to the bottom of this. Where's the key?"

"I have one." Albertini rummaged in his dressing table drawer and produced a key ring. "But I'm sure you won't find anything. The trunk was completely empty this morning when I . . ." He paused, glancing at Max and Mr. Wigglesworth. Max remembered how the trunk had grunted when Sid kicked it.

". . . when I used it," finished the magician.

"Let's find out," said Officer Todd. He fit the key into the padlock and twisted it hard. The lock popped open. Everyone stepped closer as the officer lifted the lid.

The trunk was empty.

Caught Red-Handed

"Where's Sid?" cried Max. He grabbed Dad's arm. "I left her in there, I swear!"

Dad stared at him. "You left Sid in the trunk?"

"Who's Sid?" asked the officer.

"The boy is obviously insane," said Lola.

"I'm not crazy," insisted Max. He whirled around to face Lola. "Sid was in that trunk when you locked it."

Lola let out a short laugh. "So where is he now?"

"Who is this Sid fellow?" demanded Officer Todd for a second time.

"*She's* my best friend," said Max, groping for an explanation. "We were, uh, looking for something, and . . ."

"Meddling with private property," sputtered Lola. "A liar and a thief."

"Max isn't a thief," squeaked a voice.

Everyone stared into the empty trunk. For a moment nothing happened, then the bottom gave a jiggle. A second later it jerked and slid to one side. From the dark depths emerged a freckled arm, then another arm followed by a tangle of orange-red hair. Finally Sid sat up, pale and trembling. A long gold chain dangled from one ear and when she shook her head several crumpled dollar bills flew into the air.

"Good grief," gasped Mr. Wigglesworth.

"There's more," Sid smiled weakly, "in the secret compartment."

"Ah, yes," said the Amazing Albertini. "The false-bottom trunk trick. A wonderful illusion."

Officer Todd stepped forward. "I'm not sure

who you are, young lady, but you'd better have a good explanation. Theft is a serious crime."

Sid swallowed. "Explanation?" She glanced at Max. "Crime?"

Max nodded. "The audience was robbed."

"And they think I did it?" Sid looked from Max to the police officers, her eyes wide.

Lola tossed her hair. "We caught you red-handed, didn't we?"

"You've got that backwards," Max said, glaring at Lola. How had he ever thought she was beautiful? "We caught *you* red-handed. I was hiding behind the monkey cage. I heard you throw a whole bunch of stuff into the trunk."

Lola stepped toward Max, her eyes narrowing to angry slits. "You little . . ."

"Hold on, now," said Officer Todd, putting up his hand. Turning to Sid, he asked, "Did you see Lola put the stolen goods into the trunk?"

Sid shook her head. "Well, no. Not exactly."

"What?" cried Max.

"I was so scared when you closed the lid," explained Sid, "I couldn't stop shaking. I guess I must have pressed a secret button because all of a sudden I slid into this empty space at the bottom of the trunk. Then the floor snapped back and I couldn't see a thing. Just blackness!"

Max groaned. Without Sid as an eye witness, it was his word against the Lovely Lola's.

"I'm sorry, Max," said Sid with an apologetic shrug. "I heard stuff being thrown into the trunk, but I couldn't see a thing. When you went for help I found the secret button and pushed it. I wanted to see what they'd put in here. But then I heard voices again and I got scared and hid."

Officer Todd's face was solemn. Taking Sid's arm, he helped her out of the trunk. "I'm afraid we're going to have to take you in for questioning, young lady."

"But I'm innocent," sputtered Sid. "Tell them, Max!"

Max couldn't believe what was happening. Once again, his big idea had backfired. All he had wanted was to be rich, and now Sid was going to jail. He turned to Dad. "We didn't steal anything, I swear. You've got to believe me."

"Don't worry, kids." Mr. Wigglesworth shoved his notepad into his pocket and put his arms around Max's and Sid's shoulders.

"We'll straighten this out."

"Down at the station," added Officer Todd. He nodded to Officer Perkins. "Bring them all. The kids too."

"Surely that's not necessary," protested Dad. "This is all a big misunderstanding . . ."

Just then a spine-tingling shriek filled the air. Everyone turned to the monkey cage, which had begun to shake. The sheet quivered, then slipped to the floor, revealing Shimmy with his tiny fingers wrapped around the bars. He shrieked again and began jumping up and down like an angry jack-in-the-box.

"Watch out," cried Max, pointing at Shimmy. "He's got something in his hand!"

A small object whizzed across the room, hit Dad in the head and fell to the floor with a splat. It was a wad of chewed gum.

"Hey," yelped Dad. He wiped his forehead and then stared at the slimy spot on his hand.

"He's got something else," shouted Max.

Shimmy screeched again. He rattled the bars and fired another missile. This one smacked Officer Todd in the ear before clattering to the floor and rolling under the loveseat.

"Somebody control that monkey," yelled the officer, rubbing his ear.

The Amazing Albertini hurried to the cage and opened the door. Shimmy hopped into the magician's arms and glared around the room, chattering menacingly.

"I'm really sorry," apologized Albertini. "Shimmy is usually very good with people. I trained him myself."

"A trained monkey, huh?" Officer Todd dropped to his knees and felt under the loveseat with one hand. He pulled out the object that Shimmy had hurled at him.

It was a small gold cufflink.

Officer Todd raised his eyebrows. "What, exactly, did you train him to do?"

Albertini gasped. "I don't understand. I'd never teach Shimmy to steal from people."

Max's brain buzzed again. He remembered what Lola had said when she put Shimmy in his cage.

You know the routine.

"Maybe you didn't teach him to steal, but I'll bet she did," Max cried, pointing once again at the Lovely Lola.

"Nonsense," sputtered Lola. "I'll sue you for slander, I'll press libel charges, I'll . . ."

They never found out what other horrible things Lola planned to do. Shimmy took one look at Max's outstretched arm and leaped across the room, landing on Lola's shoulder. Before she could finish her threats, he climbed down her body like it was a coconut tree and dove under her skirts.

When he popped out again, he was holding a diamond bracelet.

16 Sticky Fingers

"I knew that skirt had secret pockets," exclaimed Max. He turned to Sid. "Magicians always have something up their sleeves. Or in this case, in their skirt."

Lola snatched the bracelet and gave Shimmy a shove. "Get off me, you nasty creature," she hissed. Shimmy screeched and leapt to the safety of his cage.

"How do you explain the bracelet, Miss Lola?" asked Officer Todd.

"It's mine," she snapped.

Max stared at the bracelet. Why did it seem familiar? He furrowed his forehead, thinking hard.

"Eieee! Eieee!" Shimmy danced in a circle on top of his cage, his arms flailing excitedly.

"Mommy, I saw a monkey," shouted Max, suddenly remembering.

Everyone looked at Max.

"Uh, your mom isn't here," whispered Sid.

"No," said Max, "that's what the little boy

said in the theater. His mom was upset because her diamond bracelet was stolen, and he tried to tell her that he saw a monkey. She thought he meant on stage, in the show. But he really meant he saw a monkey take the bracelet. Nobody ever listens to kids."

Officer Todd frowned and scratched his head. "I'm not sure a monkey could wander through an audience filled with people and only be noticed by one small child."

"My show is quite entertaining," offered the Amazing Albertini.

Officer Todd nodded slowly. "I'm sure it is, but still . . ."

"Hey," interrupted Sid. "Bring that back!"

Shimmy scampered over the trunk, clambered up Albertini's cape and perched on his shoulder. His tail was curled around a wrinkled paper bag.

"That's mine," protested Sid. "He stole it right out of my pocket."

Max grinned at Officer Todd. "See?"

Officer Todd shook his head. "I just don't know."

"I'm so sorry," said Albertini. He pried the bag from Shimmy's tail and handed it to Sid. Then he wrestled something from Shimmy's clenched fist and gave it to Officer Todd. "Very sorry indeed."

The officer's cheeks grew pink. "My badge," he said. He frowned and nodded to Perkins. "Find the woman and her son. Bring her here to ID the bracelet."

The room was uncomfortably quiet after Perkins left. Even Shimmy sat still. Finally Albertini broke the silence.

"Why?" he asked Lola, putting a gentle hand on her arm.

Lola jerked her arm away. "Why? You dare ask me why?"

Albertini looked bewildered. "I don't understand. We've been partners for so many years. Split everything right down the middle, fifty-fifty. I thought we were a team. Why would you do this?"

"A team?" Lola leaned forward and spat her words into his face. "It's always been the Amazing Albertini and his assistant. Do you have any idea what that's like? Always the helper, never the star? I'm tired of living out of a suit-case, sick of making barely enough to cover our tickets to the next place. Ten years I've been doing this. Ten years!"

"B-but . . . I thought you loved what we do," stuttered Albertini.

Lola straightened her shoulders, her eyes glittering. "I hate it. I hate everything about it. I only took this job because I thought there was cash in it. All I wanted was enough money to retire to a tropical island somewhere. Boy, did I make a mistake."

"So you trained Shimmy to be a thief?" questioned Officer Todd.

Lola shrugged. "The monkey has always had sticky fingers, if you know what I mean. I just taught him how to use them. We've been doing it for years. Just one or two items per show. Not enough to arouse suspicion. Shimmy never had any trouble slipping under the seats, looking for open pockets or purses."

She paused and fresh tears leaked down her cheeks. "I've been saving all these years. I just needed one last big haul and I could have run away and lived a life of leisure. One last job."

"So you're the one who hit me?" Albertini

touched his forehead, which was sticky with blood.

"Yes," said Lola. She spoke dully now, staring straight ahead. "I hit you and tied you up. Then I tied myself up. I've learned a trick or two with rope over the years. I had to make it look like I was a victim too."

"And the loot?" prompted Officer Todd.

"It was safe enough in the false-bottom trunk," replied Lola. "All I had to do was wait until the heat died down, then I'd collect it and flee the country. It was the perfect plan." She glared at Max and Sid. "And it would have worked if it hadn't been for those two."

17 Back to Normal

"Knock, knock," said Max, pushing open the heavy hospital door. "Can we come in?"

"Enter," commanded a voice.

Max grinned at Sid as they stepped inside the small private room. He held out a bouquet of delphiniums Mom had cut from her garden this morning. "These are for you."

The Amazing Albertini was sitting up in bed. He looked a little tired. A thick white bandage wound around his forehead and he wore a flimsy cotton hospital gown. But his voice was as deep and rich as ever.

He waved toward the room's only window. "Thank you, they're beautiful. Why don't you set them over there."

While Sid arranged the flowers in an empty vase, Max dragged a chair next to the magician's bed and sat down. "How do you feel?"

Albertini flashed a stage smile. "Better. My head will be sore for awhile, but I'll be back to performing before you know it."

"You're going to keep doing your show?" asked Max. "What about the Lovely Lola?"

"I'm afraid she'll be unavailable for the next few years. I guess I'll have to find another assistant," Albertini said. He looked sad for a moment, then shrugged. "I had no idea she was unhappy. How could I have been so blind?"

Max had been wondering that himself. He thought about his parents and how much they loved their jobs. "Maybe it's because you were happy," he said. "Sometimes when a person does something they really, really love, it kind of takes up all their attention. It doesn't make them a bad person."

Albertini tried to smile. "I've been happy every minute of my career. It never occurred to me that Lola didn't feel the same way."

"I still have one question," Max said. He glanced over at Sid, who was fiddling with the flowers. He knew she was giving him some time alone with the magician and he was grateful.

"What is it?"

Max looked down at his hands. "At the

interview, you told me that being a magician made you wealthy beyond your wildest dreams. But Lola started stealing because she was tired of not being rich. I don't get it."

Albertini gazed out the hospital window and sighed. "I do consider myself a wealthy man," he answered slowly. "Money alone would never have brought me as much joy as being a magician does. Never. Performing illusions, adding a touch of mystery to people's lives, hearing the applause . . . these are the things that make me rich."

Sid came over to stand beside Max. "So you're not ready to retire yet?"

Albertini crossed his arms over his chest. "Not for all the money in the world," he proclaimed in his booming stage voice.

Max laughed. "Hey, since you're going to be stuck in here for awhile, can we get you anything?"

"Yeah," said Sid, looking at the uneaten food on the lunch tray beside the bed. She poked at a dish of lumpy mashed potatoes and boiled fish. "This stuff doesn't look so good."

Albertini grimaced. "I'm afraid not even a great magician like myself can transform hospital food into something edible. What I wouldn't give for a nice salami sandwich."

Max stared at the tray. Suddenly the gears began turning inside his head. Everybody hates hospital food, he thought. Mushy vegetables, unsalted eggs, gluey oatmeal . . . bland, bland, bland. Suppose someone came along selling really tasty food? Fresh sandwiches or pizza or maybe even fondue? Why, a person could make a fortune!

"Max?" repeated Sid. "Hey, Max. Are you listening?"

Max slowly focused on Sid's face. "Huh?"

Albertini chuckled. "I said that I never got a chance to thank you for all your help. You're a very smart boy and you could make a brilliant magician some day. So to thank you, I'd be willing to pass my knowledge on to you. But you'd have to practice for years and years, slowly perfecting your technique and adding to your repertoire. What do you say?"

"Uh, thanks," said Max, shaking his head, "but I don't think I'm cut out for the magic business after all. Nope," he added, the gears in his brain turning a hundred miles a minute. "If I'm going to become a millionaire, I need to come up with a really excellent idea. A brilliant scheme. The perfect plan . . ."

"Oh boy," snorted Sid, recognizing the zombie look in Max's eyes. "Where have I heard that before?"

Check out Max's other exciting adventures – now available with all new illustrations!

"Max and Sid ... have undeniable chemistry ..." – *The Horn Book*

"... just the right amount of humour and mystery."
– *CM: Canadian Review of Materials*

"... engaging and lively ..." – *Midwest Book Review*

MAX THE MIGHTY SUPERHERO
978-1-897073-95-7

Max enlists his friend Sid to go into the superhero business, in hopes of raking in the rewards. But things go haywire when the only baby they rescue has four feet and the owner has plenty to hide.

MAX THE MOVIE DIRECTOR
978-1-897073-96-4

Max thinks that he can make his millions if he directs the biggest blockbuster movie of all time. Will his Hollywood ending be jeopardized by one last plot twist?

MAX THE BUSINESSMAN
978-1-897073-93-3

Max is planning to corner the Main Street flower market, until someone murders "Victor" – a prize-winning orchid. In a flash, Max goes from gardener to detective as he tries to catch the culprit and snag a big reward in the process!